Have You Ever Zeen a Ziz?

Linda Elovitz Marshall

illustrated by Kyle Reed

Albert Whitman & Company
Chicago, Illinois

To DJB&R—the little birds who left my nest
and to the fledglings they're nurturing:
Gabriel, Niomi, Julia Rose, Avigail, Lyra, Talia,
Leah, Noa, Baruch, Ezra, Aviya, Orly, Ellie,
and those yet to hatch out—LEM

To Mom and Dad. Thanks—KR

Library of Congress Cataloging-in-Publication data is on file with the publisher.

Text copyright © 2020 by Linda Elovitz Marshall
Illustrations copyright © 2020 by Albert Whitman & Company
Illustrations by Kyle Reed
First published in the United States of America in 2020 by Albert Whitman & Company
ISBN 978-0-8075-3173-0 (hardcover)
ISBN 978-0-8075-3174-7 (ebook)

Printed in China
10 9 8 7 6 5 4 3 2 1   WKT 24 23 22 21 20 19

Design by Sarah Richards Taylor

For more information about Albert Whitman & Company,
visit our website at www.albertwhitman.com.

Have you ever *zeen* a Ziz?
Do you wonder what one
iz?

Is it *zis*?

Is it bigger than a hat?

Is it like a giant cat?

Or a prehistoric bat?

No, a Ziz is NOT like those.

It's a bird that puts on shows
as she dips from high to low
with her feathers all aglow.

Her wings span from
there to here.
Her wings **s-t-r-e-e-e-tch** from
here to there.

Ziz's wings spread
EVERYWHERE.

When the Ziz is flying by,
giant wings block out the sky.

So because she hides the light,
the Ziz *mostly*
flies by night.

She's a kindly, gentle bird.
Big and yellow,
sweet...

She stops winds and driving rains
to help farmers grow their grains.

When she stands upon the land
with her heels dug into sand,

her head rests upon a cloud,
and she ZINGS
OUT
LOUD...**LOUD**...
LOUD!

She *zings* melodies and rhymes
of both happy
   and sad times.

Ziz *zings* when she's at home.
Ziz *zings* when she's alone.

Ziz *zings* when she's at play.

Ziz *zings*
at end of day.

Ziz *zings* inside her nest,
where she goes to take a rest

and gaze upon creation
from her very lofty station.

When she takes a little *shluffy*,
her feathers—they get puffy.
'cause she snores and snores and *snores*,
sounding like **SIX** dinosaurs.

No snore differs,
all same-same:
Zzzzzz...Zzzzzz...Zzzzzz,
Zzzzzz...Zzzzzz...Zzzzzz.
Is that *how*
Ziz got her name?

Should you ever
zee
a Ziz...

You will know
just what one *iz*...

She's a kindly, giant bird...
Yes, a bird a bit absurd.

If you cannot
see the sky...

Could a Ziz be flying by?

Author's Note

I have never *zeen* a Ziz, but neither did I make it up. The Ziz is a mythological bird found in a collection of ancient Jewish writings. Ziz is mentioned in Psalm 50:11—"I know all the birds of the mountains and Ziz is mine" and in Psalm 80:13-14—"The boar from the forest ravages it, and Ziz feeds on it."

Bigger than all other creatures of the air (much like the leviathan is bigger than all other creatures of the sea), the Ziz is so large that when its feet touch the ground, its head reaches the clouds.

According to legend, if a Ziz egg were to fall out of the nest and break, it could cause a flood so damaging that hundreds of trees would fall and entire towns would be destroyed. As a result, the Ziz is very careful with her eggs.

My main source of information about the Ziz is the first volume of *Legends of the Jews* by Louis Ginzberg (1909), translated by Henrietta Szold.

But since I've never actually *zeen* a Ziz, I'm just guessing what one *iz*.

Author's Note

I have never *zeen* a Ziz, but neither did I make it up. The Ziz is a mythological bird found in a collection of ancient Jewish writings. Ziz is mentioned in Psalm 50:11—"I know all the birds of the mountains and Ziz is mine" and in Psalm 80:13-14—"The boar from the forest ravages it, and Ziz feeds on it."

Bigger than all other creatures of the air (much like the leviathan is bigger than all other creatures of the sea), the Ziz is so large that when its feet touch the ground, its head reaches the clouds.

According to legend, if a Ziz egg were to fall out of the nest and break, it could cause a flood so damaging that hundreds of trees would fall and entire towns would be destroyed. As a result, the Ziz is very careful with her eggs.

My main source of information about the Ziz is the first volume of *Legends of the Jews* by Louis Ginzberg (1909), translated by Henrietta Szold.

But since I've never actually *zeen* a Ziz, I'm just guessing what one *iz*.